AUT
Adventure

Part 6 of the Summer Unplugged Series

Amy Sparling

ISBN-13: 978-1512151657
ISBN-10: 1512151653

Cover art from shutterstock.com
Cover design by Amy Sparling
First edition April 2nd, 2015

Chapter 1

This might be the first night of my first (and only) honeymoon, but as I walk onto the private jet my new husband has rented for the occasion and run my fingers along the smooth vanilla-colored leather of the seat next to me, I am absolutely positive that this is the best honeymoon in the world. Not even a Kardashian could top this. I mean, yeah they're all vastly more wealthy than Jace and I will ever be, but there's one thing I have that the Kardashian clan doesn't.

Jace Adams.

I plunk down into one of the six massive seats on the jet. I'm still in my wedding gown and once my body sinks into the plush chair, exhaustion overtakes me.

"This chair must be straight from heaven because it is so freaking comfortable," I say, closing my eyes and running my hands up and down the armrests. Jace sits in the chair across from me, swiveling until our feet touch. "No sleeping just yet, Mrs. Adams," he says, smiling when he calls me by my new last name. "You have to choose our first destination so we can tell the pilot where to take us."

Did I mention that Jace has carved out three entire weeks from his work schedule so that we can spend a full twenty one days traveling around the country, doing whatever we want as we celebrate our wedding? Yeah, because that's currently happening. Suck it, every other honeymoon ever.

I toss my head back and look at the ceiling of the jet, squishing my lips to the side of my mouth while I try to think of a place to go. Up until a few moments ago, our honeymoon destination had been a secret because Jace was wanting to surprise me. I figured he had planned a trip to a beach resort or something, but as usual, what he actually planned far exceeded my expectations. He rented the jet, which came with his long time pilot friend, and gave me the reigns. Now, fear overwhelms me as I struggle to think of somewhere to go. When you have the entire country as an option, it's hard to choose.

Finally, I get an idea.

"Los Angeles!"

Jace's head tilts to the side quizzically. "LA? Why?"

I shrug. "Well, when we went to visit your parents, I had all these visions of going to LA and seeing the Hollywood sign and stuff, and then we didn't do that at all because they lived in San Francisco."

"And you had absolutely no knowledge of the geography of the state of California," Jace says with a laugh. "LA isn't really as cool as it looks in the movies, but, if that's where my wife wants to go…"

I nod enthusiastically. "Please, can we? I want to see some celebrities!"

Jace laughs and then walks up to the front of the plane, sliding open a door to the cockpit. "Take us to LA," he says, followed by, "Yep. That LA."

When he returns, he leans over and gives me a kiss before taking his seat again. "What did that mean?" I ask, referring to his conversation with Christopher, our pilot.

"He just flew in here from LA, so he thought it was funny that I told him to go right back there," Jace says. He yawns, which makes me yawn, too. It's been a long freaking day. I mean, when I woke up this morning I was still a single woman. Now I'm married.

I groan. "I'm sorry I picked LA. It's actually kind of a stupid place to go first."

Jace shakes his head. "No way. This is a spontaneous trip. Your first choice is the best one because it's what you really want. We're going and it'll be awesome."

I smile and grab his hand from across the small aisle between our chairs. "So what's behind that other door?" I ask, gesturing to the door behind us. "Is it the bathroom? Because I'm sure I'll have to pee before we get there." At the sudden thought of how much soda I had at our wedding, my eyes go wide as panic makes my stomach tighten. "Please tell me there's a bathroom in there?"

Jace laughs and shakes his head, standing up and walking toward the door. "Babe, there's a lot more than a bathroom back there." He pulls open the door with a flourish of his hand and suddenly I'm on my feet in my wedding gown, my mouth open like I'm some kind of fish underwater.

"Oh, my God," I murmur, making my way to the door. Behind it is a luxurious living room area. A flat screen television, a couch in the same fancy leather as the seats, a fully-stocked bar, a sink, and another door that probably leads to the bathroom. Jace opens it and I follow him.

Nope, it doesn't lead to the bathroom. It leads to a bedroom. A queen sized bed with a big fluffy duvet that looks as soft as a cloud. Another television, and then another door. That one leads to a bathroom.

"Wow, this place is amazing." Somehow, the

words manage to come out of my mouth despite its sudden problem with staying open in awe and fascination. "We don't even have to fly anywhere," I say, sitting on the bed which is just as comfortable as I had imagined it would be. "Let's just stay in this plane for three weeks."

Jace's gaze turns seductive at the thought of what I'd just said. He walks toward me slowly, stopping when he's in front of me while I sit on the bed. I look up at him and give him my best seductive look in return. He better be thinking what I'm thinking.

Just in case he's not, I reach up and start unbuttoning his dress shirt. I have to stand up as I get to the buttons on his chest and when I reach the top one, Jace slips his arms around my back, tugging the ribbon corset bow that's tied at the base of my dress.

A second later, my dress loosens as he works his fingers through the ribbons, making the bust of the dress begin to fall outward. I slide my fingers up his chest, feeling his rock hard abs as I push aside his shirt and let it fall to the ground.

It's funny how my incredibly expensive gown took my mom and best friend thirty minutes to put on, and only needs thirty seconds for Jace to have it pooled on the floor around my feet. I help him remove the strapless contraption that is my form-fitting bra, and then Jace lowers me onto the bed, sliding his body slowly up mine until our eyes meet. My skin tingles at the touch of his, a sensation I doubt I will ever get used to, no matter how long we're together.

"I'm so glad you married me," Jace whispers

before kissing me. My hands travel up his biceps, which are rigid while he supports his weight on top of me. His arms aren't the only hard thing I'm thinking about right now.

I bite my lip, trying to hold back the desire coursing through me, but then Jace dips his head into my neck, kissing my flesh delicately at first, then with passion as his tongue grazes across my skin, down to my collarbone. Chills prickle over every inch of my skin, and my fingers dig into his back.

"I'm glad I married you, too," I whisper, shuddering as Jace's fingers slide down my side, stopping when he grabs my hip. I draw in a deep breath as I feel him press against me. My lips touch his ear, and I make my request between gasping for air. "I'm yours, Jace. So take me."

Chapter 2

The weather in California must be the same temperature as it is in heaven year-round. Unlike the scorching hot, hair-wrecking humid conditions in Texas during this time of year, Los Angeles is a perfect seventy-two degrees with clear, sunny skies. We step out of the plane at the private airstrip near LAX and I let my head fall back, as my eyes close and I take in the beautiful weather. Already, my hair looks amazing with the low humidity. And it hasn't even been washed yet.

Jace rents a car and we hang out in the front seat, still parked at the airport while we try to figure out a place to stay.

"Just about every hotel in LA will be awesome," Jace says, leaning over to look at my phone screen as I search for hotels. "Do you have anything in mind?"

I shake my head. My ignorance of just about everything is starting to make me sad. Jace is so worldly and experienced and I just suck at everything.

"You okay?" he asks, nudging me in the shoulder with his chin.

"Yeah, I'm fine," I say, continuing to scroll on my phone.

"Liar, liar," he says. He takes my hand and I look up at him. He's wearing a blue Oakley shirt and jeans and yet he looks just as gorgeous today as he did in his tuxedo last night. I can't help but smile when I look into his gorgeous eyes. I sigh. No sense in keeping things from him—he'd only find them out eventually.

"I just feel so stupid not knowing anything

about, well, anything, and you're so smart and have been everywhere and know everything."

"That is so not true, babe. I'm not smarter than you are. Not by a long shot." I give him a sarcastic look but he keeps talking. "I know motocross and California and that's about it. Everything else in life, we'll get to learn together. I mean, I'm psyched for us to have our baby and buy a house but I have absolutely no idea how to do either one of those things."

"Really, Jace?" I say sarcastically, giving him a look. "You don't know how to have a baby?" I pat my belly, which is still pretty small but growing every day. "Seems like you did a pretty good job in knocking me up, so I think you know a little bit about the subject."

He starts laughing and reaches over, putting his hand on top of mine on my stomach. "You know what I mean. Once this kid comes out of here, I'll have no idea what to do."

"Something tells me you'll figure it out," I say, unable to hide my smile.

We search for hotels again, and then something catches my eye. "The Pink Palace?" I scroll some more and read about the Beverly Hills Hotel, a famous and legendary hotel that's over a hundred years old. And the best part? It's pink. I read aloud from the website, "It's located in the center of Beverly Hills and is surrounded by tropical gardens and exotic flowers. Oh my God, Jace," I say, looking over at him.

"That sounds amazing," he says. "Let's go." He types the hotel's name into our rental car's GPS and I buckle my seatbelt, smiling ear to ear as I get ready to drive down the famous streets of Hollywood for the first time in my life.

I wish I could say that driving through California and checking into our hotel, which is actually what they call a private bungalow, was an amazing experience that I'll remember for a lifetime. Instead, I fell asleep the second we pulled out of the airport.

I wake up some time later when Jace has my car door open and is reaching for my hand.

"Was I asleep?" I ask stupidly as I let him pull me from the car. We changed clothes on the plane, but I was so tired from the day's activities that I only had the energy to don a pair of yoga pants and a blue tank top with rhinestones along the neckline. Ugh, that is so not clothing good enough for Cali-freaking-fornia!

Jace laughs. "Sleeping? More like in a mini-coma."

We walk through an astounding garden filled with exotic plants. The floral scent overwhelms me and makes me wish I could bottle it all up and make it a perfume. For all I know, that might have already been done. I make a mental note to go shopping for fragrances in LA before we leave.

Jace opens the door to our suite and guides me to the bed. It's a four-poster, canopied and piled high with the most luxurious sheets and down comforter you could imagine. But I don't even have time to admire the way the bed closes around me like a cloud, because I fall asleep just moments after my head hits the pillow.

I wake to the smell of coffee. Jace and Becca, though I love both of them to death, are crazy addicted to coffee. I'm only a partial fan of the drink, probably because I usually fill my cup with lots of sugar and cream and then drink entirely too much and I become jittery for the rest of the day.

Luckily, I'm nearing five months pregnant and my morning sickness is just about gone. Jace must know that, or else he's forgotten because he hasn't made coffee in front of me in a while because it'd make me puke the moment I smelled it.

I open my eyes and stretch out my tired limbs, admiring once more how ridiculously soft and fluffy the sheets are. I wonder if they let you buy them from the hotel.

"Good afternoon, Sunshine!" Jace calls from across our bungalow. I can't immediately see him because this isn't just a regular hotel room — it's like an apartment that's a thousand times better than the real apartment we live in back home. I sit up on my elbows and scan the bungalow, finally finding Jace in the kitchenette, spooning sugar into his coffee.

He's shirtless with messy hair. Damn, a girl could get used to waking up to this.

"Did you say afternoon? What time is it?" I look at the nightstand for my phone, but it's not there. After how badly I passed out last night, I'm not sure where any of our stuff is.

Jace walks over to the bed, holding his coffee. He's wearing just a pair of black boxers and it makes my skin tingle just looking at him and how freaking hot he is. Just as quickly as I think it, my mind wanders to how fat I'm getting with the pregnancy. I can't help but frown and pull the sheets up higher, blocking my belly from view.

Jace doesn't notice my disposition change which is great because I am not in the mood to have a discussion about my many faults and how they bother me. "It's six-thirty," he says, sipping from a mug with the hotel's logo on it. He turns on the television and sits next to me on the bed.

"Six thirty at night?" I blurt out, glancing toward the window as if that can tell me anything. It's still sunny out, but it'd be sunny no matter what time of day it is. "I slept all freaking day?"

"Yep. Welcome to married life. Now we're old and boring." Jace lifts his mug as if he's making a toast with me. I punch him playfully in the arm and force myself to crawl out of bed. "I can't believe I wasted the whole day. And you're the old one, not me. I will always be younger than you, no matter what."

I stick out my tongue at him and he responds by grabbing it between his teeth. Then we're lying back on the bed, tangled up in the sheets and in each other's arms. His lips taste like coffee and sugar and his skin smells amazing. I feel a little guilty that he's had time to shower and make coffee before I woke up, but soon, Jace's hand slips my tank top over my head and I forget all about that.

Making love to my husband is the greatest thing ever.

Chapter 3

Even with all of the trips to the mall before our wedding, my entire wardrobe is too lame for our hotel, much less for the rest of California. Jace assures me that the black lacey dress I've chosen for dinner will be fine, but I feel so horribly under dressed. I have this frightening fear that every person who passes us in the hallway can instantly tell that I'm some uneducated country freak from the south.

It's because of these insecurities that we decide to have dinner at a restaurant in our hotel called The Polo Lounge. I order tortilla soup and pasta and Jace gets the filet mignon. The entire place is so fancy that I have a mini panic attack over which fork I should use. Jace, ever the handsome gentleman, laughs at me.

"Babe, you're stressing way too much about this. It's just a restaurant. No one cares which fork you use."

"Yeah, well I'm going to Google it anyway," I say, looking up the information on my phone. He may roll his eyes at me, but a few minutes later when I tell him he's using the wrong fork to eat his salad, he drops it and grabs the right one. Ha!

After dinner, we cruise through West Hollywood toward Los Angeles. It's nearing eight o'clock at night which makes it too late to do just about anything besides see a movie back at home, but Jace assures me there's still plenty to do in LA.

We walk hand in hand down the Walk of Fame and Jace takes pictures of me with the stars of Kaley Cuoco and Jim Parsons, two of my favorite actors. We visit a few museums and then grab a late night burger at In-and-Out and eat them in our rental car.

"This is pretty good," I say between bites.

Jace nods and stuffs more fries in his mouth. "They should totally expand into Texas. I miss these things, bad."

It's late, but we're still wide awake from our weird wedding hangover sleep fest, so I only have to beg a little bit to convince Jace to take us to the beach. The drive is a little long, but and cruising down Santa Monica Boulevard has me singing the song All I Wanna Do by Sheryl Crow.

When we get to the beach, I rush down the sand, eager to put my toes in the water. We have a beach in Texas, but the water is muddy brown and the sand is often full of old seaweed. It looks nothing like the beautiful Pacific coast.

"I wouldn't do that if I were you," Jace calls out as he jogs along behind me.

"Why not?" I call back, narrowly missing crashing into a guy throwing a Frisbee to his dog. "I have my shoes off." I wave the cheap sandals high above my head as I continue on my sprint to the water. It's a warm summer's day and all I want to do is feel the rush of the sea crashing into my feet.

"Oh holy shit!" I call out, jumping back twice as quickly as I had stepped into the water. It's freezing. Like, a melted arctic glacier freezing. "Why is it so cold?" I glare at the ocean as it crashes onto the shore, it's beautiful clear water nothing but a fake lie of coldness.

"I warned you," he says, stepping up behind me and sliding his hands around my waist. "Why do you think everyone's wearing a wetsuit around here? The Pacific ocean is cold as balls."

"Hmph." I cross my arms over Jace's while we stand in the sand just a few feet away from the water that threatens to get us with each new cresting wave. It's dark but that hasn't deterred the surfers, who to my chagrin, are definitely all wearing wetsuits. "Oh well, I guess we can go now. LA isn't really all it's cracked up to be."

"It is if you're a millionaire, I bet," Jace says.

"Everything is awesome if you're a millionaire."

"Well look at that!" Jace and I turn toward the sound of the voice that just appeared from behind us. A man about Jace's age walks toward us, holding hands with a pretty brunette girl who's wearing a dress similar to mine. "And I thought we weren't going to see a celebrity tonight!"

"Ah, man," Jace says, his face turning to a bashful smile as he approaches the guy and shakes his hand. Their gestures tell me this isn't some random stranger talking to Jace. "I'm not a celebrity," Jace says to the girl, slapping his hand on the guy's shoulder. "Whatever he's told you is a lie."

"No way, this is Jace Adams, national motocross superstar." The guy looks at me. "This must be his lovely wife."

"Wife?" I blurt out stupidly. I mean, way to just make it sound like I was embarrassed of being called that. Then I add, "How'd you know that?"

Jace's brows furrow. "How did you know that? I haven't posted it to social media yet. We've been too busy." To me, he says, "Jake Sampson, my old racing buddy from San Francisco. We used to tear up the tracks when we were kids."

Jake pulls out his cell phone, swipes the screen and then hands it to Jace. "That's how I knew, man.

Congrats by the way. I'm psyched for you."

"Are you having a baby?" the girl next to Jake asks, glancing at my stomach. She's smiling and seems sweet, so I guess she's not trying to pull a bitch move and point out how I clearly got knocked up out of wedlock. I nod, touching my stomach habitually. "Five months along now."

I look at Jace, expecting to see his trademark smile of pride that he gets every time we talk about the baby, but instead he hasn't even heard me. He's staring at Jake's phone, his features twisted into annoyance. "Who the fuck..." he murmurs, before showing me the screen.

Right there on a motocross website that often features Mixon Motocross Park and other popular race tracks, is a picture of Jace and me just twenty four hours ago at our wedding. We're holding hands and walking back down the aisle after having just said our vows. We're smiling and not looking anywhere near the camera. Someone in the audience took this photo when we weren't paying attention. And then they gave it to a website.

"Who would do this?" I ask, looking at Jace as if he'd have an answer. He shakes his head and gives the phone back to Jake. "I mean, it's not a secret or anything but it's weird. We had wanted to have our honeymoon privately and not make a big deal about the wedding. I even lied to my clients about why I took off work for three weeks," Jace says.

Jake shrugs. "It probably wasn't done out of spite. You know how reporters are, they're always asking anyone connected to celebrities to sell them photos or information."

"I am not a celebrity!" Jace says for what feels

like the millionth time in the last few weeks. "God I wish those magazines would leave me alone."

"Tough break, bro," Jake says. "I was never fast enough to have that problem. People don't give a shit about me."

"I do!" the girl says, tugging on his arm.

"This is Clara, my girlfriend," he says, wrapping an arm around her shoulder. "Sorry it took me so long to introduce you. I was star struck in front of this massive celebrity."

Jace laughs. "I hope you meet a real celebrity tonight and not a phony one like me."

Clara shakes her head. "All of my girlfriends know who you are, so you're kind of famous even if you hate it. I recognize you, as well," she says to me. "I see your picture on the motocross Facebook pages and stuff. You're friends with Hana Fisher, right?"

I nod slowly. "How do y'all know that?" I ask, looking up at Jace. "We're not really famous, are we? I mean… you don't even race professionally anymore."

"But he trains the professionals," Jake interrupts. "And he had a pretty big reputation before he moved to Texas. Maybe not famous to everyone in the country, but anyone who knows anything about motocross knows Jace Adams."

Jace nods at this. "Don't worry, babe. It's only motocross people who know us. We just happened to run into my old racing buddy."

"I sure hope so," I say with a little shudder that's not from the chill in the air. "I don't like the idea of being recognized, or talked about on websites."

Clara smiles. "I think it's cool. I'd love to be famous even if it's only mildly famous."

"I used to think that," I admit. "But seeing a picture of my own wedding on some website kind of freaks me out. At least they didn't say anything bad." I look up at Jace. "Wait, did they say anything bad?"

He shrugs. "There might have been a mention of you looking pregnant," he says without any emotion. "But it's our life so fuck them. I'm going to find out who sent that photo to the press and kick their ass."

"Let me know if you need any help, bro." Jake shakes his hand again and we all start heading back to where our cars are parked. Sadly, my desire to hang out at the beach until midnight has been ruined my the overwhelming feeling that we're being watched even when we don't realize it.

Clara lets go of her boyfriend's hand to take a place next to me. "I wouldn't worry too much," she says in a quiet, comforting voice. "The only people who would recognize you are girls who are jealous that you got to marry someone they have a crush on. It's not like anyone thinks badly of you. They're just jealous. Screw them."

"Thanks. It's weird thinking that people have a crush on my husband and they've never met him." As soon as the words are out of my mouth, I realize how weird it really is. I've always been annoyed at how girls at the motocross track flirt with him and beg for pictures with him so they can post it online. But that's a little different, because at least they've met the man they're crushing on. Realizing that tons of girls across the country like Jace and they have only seen him in pictures in motocross magazines is just weird.

Clara's smile turns devious. "Enjoy it while you can. Isn't it fun to have something everyone else wants?"

I roll my eyes. "You're fun. I like you."

"I like you, too," she says. "You're way nicer than you seem online."

I start to ask her what the hell she means by that, but we've arrived at our car and Jace and Jake start laughing at whatever they had been talking about.

"It's been good catching up," Jace says, going in for one of those handshake, pat-on-the-back things that guys do. "I'll call you next time we're in San Fran."

"Cool, cool," Jake says. He walks over to us and wraps his arm around Clara's neck, pulling her in for a kiss.

Jace opens the door of a shiny red car for me. It takes a second for me to realize this is our car, since I'm so used to Jace's massive truck. But of course we don't have the truck—we're in California on our honeymoon. Funny how hearing some drama about my life online can almost make me completely forget where I am and what I'm doing.

I wish it were enough for me to come back to reality, forget about things that might be on the internet just waiting for me to find them, and join my honeymoon with Jace, thinking of nothing but him.

But it's not that easy.

Chapter 4

Back at our hotel, Jace and I order dessert from room service and pig out in our fantastic hotel room. Diving into a massive hot fudge sundae is so much fun, I don't even have to fake being happy and normal. But as soon as my handsome husband falls asleep after we make love, I carefully crawl out of bed.

Jace's tablet is buried inside a protective sleeve at the bottom of his suitcase. It takes forever for me to quietly unzip the suitcase without waking him up. Then I fish around in the dark for the tablet and sneak it into the bathroom where the bright screen won't be as noticeable.

Staring at the tablet's search engine, I pause to ask myself if I really want to do this. Jace is famous in the motocross world and I've known that since I first met him. Usually it only bothers me when random girls rush up to him and beg for his autograph or to take a picture with him. That doesn't even bother me very much anymore. I am his wife, after all. Who cares about other girls?

Now though, after the talk with Clara on the beach, I am dying to know about the leaked picture of our wedding and to find out what people are saying about me online. I know I shouldn't do it. I know if I were to call Becca right now she would tell me to throw the tablet across the room and ignore my urges to snoop online. Because it's something like three in the morning here, and even later back in Texas, I know I can't call Becca. So with her wise words muffled by my excuse not to call her, I type in my name and Jace's name and hit search.

The first thing that comes up is a Facebook page for Texas Motocross, the biggest motocross news source and fan page for our region. Jace's boss always has banners up at the track that advertise this website and I know Jace does a ton of interviews for them.

My heart pounds as I scroll down the page but I find some relief when I see that the first post isn't anything about us. Neither is the second, or third post. I keep scrolling, my eyes glazing over wall posts from local riders and stupid pictures that random people have posted.

Finally, something appears on the screen that pertains to me. Which sucks especially bad because even though I had been looking for it, a part of me had hoped I wouldn't find anything. It's the leaked photo of our wedding. It appears to have been taken from the right side of the wedding guests because Jace and I are to the left, walking down the aisle. It's so weird that someone would do this and send a picture to the news. I mean, why? It's not like we're some crazy celebrity couple that's known for scandals.

Jace had a lot of motocross friends at the wedding, so although the photo leaker could have been anyone, I'm betting it was one of them.

I glance up at myself in the bathroom mirror, face glowing from the light of the tablet's screen. Is this stupid? Sneaking off in the middle of the night on my honeymoon just to look at gossip online?

Yes, I decide. It is most definitely stupid.

But am I above it?

Nope!

I click on the photo so I can read the comments.

There are a bunch of friendly congratulations comments and the random oddball comment that has nothing to do with the photo. And then I see words that make my knees shake.

Why did he settle for that skank? Ugh, he can do so much better.

That comment got a dozen likes and someone else had replied to it with an even worse comment: I heard she got knocked up and forced him into it.

Another comment says: I hope he got a prenup!

One particularly fantastic one says: My God, that man can get any woman he wants and he chose her?

I look at the photos of the people posting these rude things about myself — they're all women about my age. So maybe Clara was right about them just being jealous. Still, it hurts to read terrible things about myself.

Yet for some reason, I keep reading.

A few older people said they don't understand why people get married so young.

One person, whose profile photo is of a dog, said: smh. It's a shame to see young people throwing their lives away by getting married so young. They have their whole life ahead of them!

Uh, yeah, idiot. I have my whole life ahead of me and all I want to do is spend it with Jace. So why wouldn't I get married? Ugh. It takes everything I have not to reply to these comments. This tablet is logged in to Jace's account so it'd look like my bitchy rantings were coming from him and that would totally not help the situation.

Before I know it, nearly an hour has gone by and I've skimmed all twelve hundred and sixteen comments on the post. At least half, if not a little more than half of the comments are fairly nice or neutral. The rest of them say something mean or negative and a small handful are downright awful.

Although I shouldn't care one bit about what the public thinks of my marriage to Jace, if I did care, then I should be happy that most people are nice about it. Still, I feel the pull of an emotional knot in my stomach as I turn off the tablet and sneak back into our hotel room. Jace is still asleep, breathing deeply and probably dreaming about a world that's peaceful and stress-free. I wish I could be like him. I wish I could ignore things that bother me and focus on the good.

Sometimes Jace seems so completely perfect in every possible way. I wonder if he's faking it?

When I hide the tablet back where it was and crawl into bed as quietly as I can, Jace's breathing hitches and he rolls over closer to me. I use the movement he makes as a way to hurry up and slide under the sheets without him noticing. He doesn't wake up, and his breathing falls back into a steady rhythm in a few seconds. Now he's facing me, one arm under his head and the other one on top of my hand.

When people sleep, their faces get a chance to fully rest. People look serene and even happy while they sleep. The thing about Jace is, as I look at him in the dim light of the hotel room, his face looks exactly as serene as it always does. Maybe Jace isn't faking his happiness at all. Maybe he truly has found a way to be happy with himself and his life and forget about what everyone else thinks.

I hope someday I can be exactly like him.

Chapter 5

After four days of shopping on Beverly Hills Boulevard, looking for celebrities (of which we found none) and taking pictures of the Hollywood sign, I kind of just want something that reminds me of home. Luckily, Jace agrees and we hit up the first McDonald's we find on the way back to the airport.

I haven't told him about what I looked up on the tablet last night. As far as he knows, neither one of us have been checking social media at all. After all, this is our honeymoon. We almost didn't bring the tablet at all, but then Jace got worried that he might have some work emails or something urgent come up, so we brought it just in case.

Not only had I stayed up later than Jace to snoop online, I'd also woken up about an hour earlier than he did. I used this time to stare at the gorgeous silk canopy above our heads and practice the art of telling myself to be cool. Okay, maybe it wasn't as lame as that sounds, but I just focused on good thoughts and tried to push out all of the bad things I'd read online, things like being called a skank and ugly. I think it helped a little.

And now as I walk into McDonald's with Jace by my side, I glance over at him for the millionth time today and smile. He is all mine. He doesn't think I'm a skank or ugly. He thinks the world of me. Yeah, maybe he's messed up in the head for thinking that and maybe I totally don't deserve him, but guess what, bitches online? I got him!

"What's that look for?" Jace asks, nudging me in the ribs with his elbow. "Are you that obsessed with McDonald's?

"What are you talking about?" I ask.

He shakes his head and stares at me, contemplating something. "I don't know…for a second there you looked like…well like you were going to kick some ass. And it was when you were looking at the menu, so...yeah, you're weird."

I laugh. "I wasn't looking at the menu like that, I was just thinking those things to my head."

"And what thoughts are in your head?" he asks, bumping into me in this purposefully annoying way that he does while we stand in line behind an older woman.

I shrug. "You know. Thoughts."

"Aww, come on! I wanna know." With record speed, he juts out his bottom lip as if he was a gold medalist in the game of puppy faces.

I roll my eyes and step forward in line. It's our turn to order, which makes this even more fun because now he can suffer while he waits to find out what I was thinking. I order a coffee, two hash browns, a set of hotcakes and then a third hash brown for good measure. What can I say? I'm eating for two now and I won't let the opportunity to eat pass me by.

Jace orders the biggest breakfast meal they have and he doesn't say a word about my embarrassingly huge food order and it makes me love him even more. When we sit down to eat, I shove half a hash brown in my mouth and roll my eyes back at how good it is. "Gourmet five-star restaurant food is good and all, but nothing beats this kind of comfort food."

"Truth," Jace says with a nod. "Although your lazy nachos are pretty good, too."

Lazy nachos are what I call one of my most

embarrassing snack food concoctions. It's where I fill a plate with tortilla chips, then dump a bunch of shredded cheese on top and nuke it all in the microwave for thirty seconds. It's about as lazy and pathetic as you can get, but as a teenager with a hungry stomach and zero cooking skills, it's a lifesaver.

I was so embarrassed the first time Jace came over and caught me making some. I almost left them in the microwave until he left, but of course, he smelled them and opened the microwave himself. Then, not only did he not make fun of me, he gave me a tip: if you use a glass plate instead of a paper plate, then the cheese won't stick to the paper and you get to eat more of it.

Yep. He's a keeper.

"Sorry I'm eating such an embarrassingly huge amount of food," I say sheepishly, as I start in on my second hash brown and open the syrup for my hotcakes. "I don't know why, but I'm freaking starving. Hopefully no one you know will see us."

Jace cocks his head to the side, staring at me while he finishes chewing the food in his mouth. "That is not a lot of food," he says, motioning toward my side of the booth. "Plus you're eating for two. So, eat up. I want my son big and strong." He winks at me as he takes another bite but his reassurances mean nothing.

"I hope I don't get really fat with this pregnancy," I say, feeling the thoughts manifest so strongly in my mind that now I suddenly don't want to eat anymore. "I should have ordered fruit or something. God," I mutter under my breath as I start to push the tray of food away. "I'm going to get disgusting."

"Honey," Jace says, reaching for my arm.

"No." I pull away. "Don't say honey and then make me feel better. You can't make me feel better when I just realized that my terrible eating is going to make me a fat gross cow."

Jace leans back in the booth seat, resting his hands behind his head while I go on for a few more sentences of self-loathing and shaming.

"Are you done?" he asks a moment later.

"I guess," I mutter, desperately wanting to grab for that third hash brown.

"Well make sure you're done, because I have something to say and I don't want you to shush me."

I roll my eyes. "Fine, I'm done."

He's quiet for a moment and finally he says, "I love you. Do you know what that means? It doesn't just mean that I love you at the moment I say it. It means I love you forever, in all aspects. Even when you're being a jerk to me, or when you've stolen the remote and make me watch stupid TV shows. Do you get what I'm saying?"

I nod. "I love you, too. I don't really see your point."

He leans forward and reaches for my hand. I allow him to take it but it's hard for me to look him in the eyes. I'm too busy feeling gross and fat. "Bayleigh, my love for you will always be here. If you're fat or if you're skinny — I'll still love you."

"You don't know that," I snap, only to be cut off with a sharp gaze from my husband. "I said it, so it's true," he says. "And I'm serious. First of all, you're halfway into a pregnancy and we both know your body will get bigger because there's a baby in there," he says with a smile, which makes me smile, too. "We already read all the stuff about pregnancy. Your ankles will get swollen, your stomach will get huge — pretty much everything that is sucky is going to happen to you. That's just life and it's all natural and if you think for one second that you're gross because of it, then you're wrong. I think it's awesome that we're having a kid. And I'm sorry I get to stay all handsome and you have to go through labor."

He smirks when he calls himself handsome and I roll my eyes. "I'm sorry, too. I wish you were the one getting fat and disgusting while I just sat back and watched."

"Bay, you're not fat and disgusting."

I look down at my lap. "I feel like it."

"Eat your food. You have nothing to worry about."

"Yeah I do," I say, looking with contempt toward the remaining hash brown and hotcakes. "What if my eating habits stay this bad and I stay fat even after the baby is born?"

"So what?" he says.

I pull my hand away from his and cross my arms. "So what?" I say, mocking him. "You can't say so what. My whole life is at stake here. I can't lose you. We have to start eating better."

"You're not going to lose me, babe. You can gain weight and it's not going to make me stop loving you."

Arms still folded, I shake my head and look away. "You're such a liar."

"Don't call me that. I would never lie to you."

"Looks like you just did. You wouldn't stay with me if I was fat. Not when you could have any pick of any woman you want."

"Bayleigh, is that really what you think? Even now, when we're married and made vows to each other and are having a kid together, you really think that I would just walk away from all of that just because you gained weight?"

I nod. "I don't know why you wouldn't."

He sighs and shakes his head. "I love you too much for that and I wish you knew it."

I sigh, too, although mine is out of resentment for myself and not over Jace. "I know you mean well, babe. But I know what other girls think about you. There are so many girls out there who are way hotter than I'll ever be. It puts a lot of pressure on me to stay good enough for you. Sure, I can get fat now with the baby but once he's born I'll have to bust my ass to get hot for you again. It's just a lot to worry about. I know you don't mean to ever leave me, but you might think twice about that when the time comes."

Jace takes a long sip of his drink and then reaches across the table with his fork and steals a bite of my hotcakes. "Have you ever seen my mom in a bathing suit?"

"You know I haven't," I say, recalling the one and only time I met his parents a few months ago, if you don't count the wedding. No one was wearing swimwear at our wedding. "What's your point?"

"One day I'm sure we'll all go swimming together," he says. "Probably next summer since they'll be begging to hang out with their grandkid. You'll see her in a bathing suit and you'll probably wonder what everyone else, including me, wonders."

"What's that?" I ask, afraid to know the answer.

Jace's mom isn't a supermodel, but for a middle-aged woman, she's not ugly either. She's neither fat nor skinny, but a nice average size. But if she's anything like my mom, she will refuse to be seen in a bathing suit in public.

"She used to be morbidly obese," Jace says, knocking all of my ideas out of the water. That is the last thing I expected him to say.

"Seriously?" I blurt out.

He nods. "For like, my whole childhood. All she ever did was complain about being fat and gross and I grew up thinking that's how all women were. I didn't think my mom was gross, but she pretty much convinced me she was with how much she said it."

"What happened?" I ask. I barely know the woman but now I'm dying to know her story.

"So Dad was always gone on business and I was always on a dirt bike, so our family barely had any quality time together. But one day we were all free on the same weekend because my race had rained out, so Mom planned this family BBQ dinner thing and said I could invite some friends over to go swimming. So anyhow, everyone was swimming except my mom because she refused to be seen in a bathing suit, but we were all having fun." Jace smiles as he recalls the memory and I see him for the first time as a little kid in my mind. He continues, "Dad was getting pretty drunk, because he can't grill unless he's drinking and they were grilling a ton of food. At one point, I was walking inside to go pee and I overheard my parents talking. I don't think they had any idea I was in the next room. Dad told her she should go swim and enjoy the water and she said no because the last bathing suit she bought was a size thirty and she didn't think it fit her anymore. And then Dad said 'You know you were a size two when we first met' and I was like oh shit, this is it. Dad's about to be murdered."

Jace stops to laugh and shake his head. My eyes are almost bugging out of my head and I urge him to go on. "Well? She obviously didn't murder him, so what happened?"

Jace shrugs. "My dad said something that's never left me. He said, 'The funny thing is that over the last twenty years, you've only gotten more beautiful.'"

Chills fill my arms. How could anyone say that and mean it? As if reading my mind, Jace says, "I believed it, too. My dad always looked at my mom like she was some kind of princess. He taught me what love is. And at that moment, even though I was like thirteen, I knew I wanted to marry someone who would be beautiful to me no matter what. Honestly, I thought that about you when we started dating. I knew a long time ago that I'd love you until the day I die."

With reluctance, I grab my fork and stab it through my breakfast. "Thank you," I say quietly. Jace's insight on life and love started years before he met me. I will have to hug his dad extra hard next time I see him. "So why did your mom lose the weight?"

Jace shrugs. "Over the next year or so, she slowly lost weight. I think she just ate better and she always took long walks around the neighborhood. I never asked her about it, but I guess she just wanted to feel as beautiful as my dad already thought she was. But now she has a lot of loose skin and she never complains about it. She doesn't mind going swimming either. She just does her thing and enjoys life and it's made her such a better person than back when all she did was complain about her looks."

I think I'll hug his mom extra hard, too.

Chapter 6

"Wake up!" I shove Jace's arm. "Jaceeeee," I say into his ear. God, if he doesn't hurry and wake up from his junk-food coma, he'll miss it. The plane jolts slightly and I grab onto the back of Jace's recliner to steady myself. He opens his eyes, furrowing his brows.

"Did we just hit turbulence?" he asks, yawning.

"That's what woke you up? Seriously?" I roll my eyes and grab his hand, pressing it to my stomach as I stand over him on the airplane.

"What are you--?" he asks, stopping the moment our baby kicks his palm. "Oh my God," he whispers, tears filling his eyes a moment later. "He's moving!"

"You can finally feel it," I say, relieved that Jace woke up in time to experience this. Until now, the baby had only moved to where I could feel it inside my body. Now, he is big enough to kick hard enough to be felt from the outside. That's what woke me up from my junk food coma, because up until a few minutes ago, I was passed out in the leather recliner next to him while our plane flies us across the country.

"This is amazing," he says, placing both hands on my stomach and moving them around, keeping up with the movement of our baby. "Oh my God, this is so cool. You see this kind of thing in the movies, but I've never actually felt it."

"Trust me, I know exactly what you mean. I'm not looking forward to the giving birth part of what I've seen in the movies…"

Jace laughs and I want to punch him in the face. "So not funny!" I snap. He closes his mouth and pretends to zip it shut. "I wonder where we are?" he asks, changing the subject to look out of the window. All I see are clouds and the ground below.

When we left LA after breakfast, I had wanted to fly to Washington but the weather was bad up there, so our pilot suggested we save that for another day. Since the hustle and bustle of LA had worn me out, I thought we should go somewhere with a nature vibe, somewhere without tall buildings and tons of cars causing traffic jams. Somewhere beautiful and warm.

So now we're headed to the Grand Canyon. Having only seen pictures of it, I am super excited to see such a huge feat of nature up close and personal. I crawl into Jace's lap, snuggling against him in the large reclining seat. "We can go back to sleep now," I murmur, resting my face against his shoulder. He wraps an arm around me and slides the other one over my stomach.

I close my eyes, feeling more content than sleepy. Jace kisses my forehead and lets his cheek rest on top of my hair. A few moments later, he nudges me. "Babe? You asleep?"

I look up, blinking and suppressing a yawn. "No, why?"

He points to the window.

We're flying over the greatest geological structure in the United States and it takes my breath away. I press my hands on either side of the window as I peer out into the vast canyon below. I think our pilot is going out of his way to give us this amazing view, because he turns the plane, making us sway to the left as he makes a wide circle around part of the canyon, giving us extra time to view its beauty.

There are mountains in California and beaches

in Texas, but this, this is more amazing than mountains and beaches. This is millions of years' worth of Mother Nature doing her thing.

"It's kind of terrifying," I say, looking over at Jace who has pressed himself against the next window. "It's so huge."

"It's amazing," he agrees. "You know," he says, tapping his chin in that way that tells me he's up to something stupid. "If my love for you were water…it would overflow this canyon in a heartbeat.

I throw my head back and roll my eyes. "I can't believe you just said something so lame! You are so cheesy!"

With a sneaky smile, Jace steps over to me and wraps his arms around me. "I'm married now. I can be as lame and cheesy as I want." I roll my eyes yet again, and he ignores my insult and kisses me instead. At first, I want to pull away from the kiss and go back to staring at the window, but then his tongue grazes across my bottom lip and suddenly I'm digging my fingers into his back, begging for more.

It's funny how that boy's tongue can get me to do almost anything.

Diving back into the kiss, I chase his tongue with mine, pulling him closer to me. He sits back in the recliner and pulls me on top of him, straddling my legs on either side of his lap. I wrap my hands around his neck and kiss him hard and soft, fast and slow. He tastes like the pack of Twizzlers we just shared and his hair smells like hotel shampoo. I love making out with him in a private jet, hundreds of miles from home.

His hands slide down my thighs, the warmth of

his skin making my legs tingle from his touch. I meet his gaze and lift an eyebrow. "Do we have time to…you know…?"

Jace smiles and glances down at my cleavage, an instinctual act that he can't stop once he's turned on. "Let's find out," he says, his voice raspy as he lifts me up a few inches so he can lean forward and kiss my chest just above my bra.

As if on cue, the plane immediately begins descending. The change in elevation makes my stomach tighten, or maybe I'm just that turned on by the idea of ripping off Jace's clothing. He slides his hands further down my thighs and around my butt, suggestively pulling me closer to his pelvis.

I bite my lip and glance out of the window. "We can't," I say, feeling the plane descend even closer to the earth. "We're about to land."

"We could try," Jace says, leaning in to kiss my neck in the spot that he knows will drive me insane. My breath catches in my throat and I want him so, so bad, but now I can actually see the runways beneath us as we get ready to land.

"I am not going to be caught having sex by our pilot." I lean back in his lap and shake my head to clear it of its naughty thoughts. "It's too risky and I would absolutely die if he caught us doing it."

Jace makes a little puppy frown, but then he sighs. "You're right. But now I don't give a shit about the Grand Canyon. Now I just want you."

"Too bad," I say playfully as I stand up and head back to my seat to buckle my seatbelt for the landing. "If you want this hot pregnant body, you'll just have to wait until tonight!"

Jace tosses his head back against his seat, staring

at the ceiling as he says, "Mean. So mean."

We fly into the Phoenix Sky Harbor International Airport and I'm surprised to find that this airport is just as busy as the one in LA. Airports are fun for me, probably because I haven't been to that many of them. At least that's what Jace says. There's a ton of interesting looking people fluttering here and there and the shops have everything from bestselling books to funky souvenirs.

There's even an electronics store selling tablets and cell phones. "Who goes to the airport to buy a cell phone?" I think aloud. Jace shrugs. "Someone who lost their phone on vacation."

While Jace rents a car, I find a kiosk with tourist brochures and grab every one they have about the Grand Canyon. We're visiting the South Rim, which as the brochures tell me, is the most popular part of the Canyon. I flip through information about helicopter tours (awesome!), white water rafting (hell no!), and hiking trails (maybe...). There are many hotels available and although I get a bit panicky trying to choose which one we should go to, it's kind of fun having a vacation with no itinerary.

"What if all of the hotels are booked up?" I ask as Jace loads our suitcases into the trunk of the rental car. The thought of being in the middle of nowhere without a place to stay is a little terrifying.

"We'll figure it out," he says, sounding zero percent worried about the ordeal. On the plus side, it's mid-August and that's when most people are getting ready to go back to school or college. It's not like it's a busy tourist season, so hopefully we'll be fine.

Besides, I'm pretty sure I can get through any problem as long as I'm with Jace.

Once we're out of the busy airport parking lot, we pull over at a café that's a combination diner and souvenir shop. From here, I spread out the hotel brochures that looked the coolest to me, and Jace and I pick a place to stay that has an onsite bowling alley and a game room.

"Not that we'll have any time to play arcade games," Jace says with a wink. "If we're at the hotel, I'll be in bed, enjoying my wife."

"I dunno," I say. "Playing some Skee-ball sounds like a lot more fun than hooking up all night…" Jace makes a pouty face and I grab the front of his shirt and pull him in for a kiss.

We set the car's GPS for our chosen hotel on the South Rim of the canyon and it calculates the route.

"Three hours?" I burst out. "Are you kidding me? We just flew over that damn canyon, how it is so far away?"

"Christopher mentioned that it was a long drive from the airport to the actual canyon," Jace says. "I thought you heard that?"

I shake my head and slip a pair of sunglasses over my eyes. "If I had known I'd be spending so much time in a car with you, maybe I would have opted out of this whole honeymoon thing." I stick out my tongue and he gives me a smirk that's so hot it makes my toes tingle.

Chapter 7

After checking in our hotel, I'm exhausted from the drive. I lean against Jace while we wait in the elevator to take us up to our new hotel room. "It's not that late," I say, bursting into a yawn. "Why am I so tired?"

"Traveling will do that to you. I'm tired, too." He wraps an arm around my waist to support me, and soon we stop on the fifth floor.

Now that we are finally near the Grand Canyon, I thought I'd be jumping up and down, begging to rush out to see it. But exhaustion has seeped into my bones and now the idea of falling onto a strange bed and sleeping for hours sounds like a dream come true.

Our hotel room isn't as fancy as the one in California, but it's clean and it smells nice and that's really all you need. I wanted to help Jace carry in our luggage, but once he opens the door with the little plastic key card, my body gets a mind of its own and walks straight to the bed, falling down on it, face first.

I wake up from a weird dream where something keeps kicking my stomach. Of course, as I stretch and yawn in the unfamiliar bed, my dream fades away and I realize the kicking sensation came from the baby inside of me, not a dream. I look around for Jace and find him sleeping, fully-clothed and on top of the sheets, next to me.

He looks so peaceful. It's a shame I'm about to wake him up.

"Hey." I nudge him in the arm but it doesn't do anything. "Jace," I whisper-yell, snuggling closer to him as I tug on his shirt. "Wake up, Sunshine!"

His eyelids flutter and he smiles, still half asleep, when he sees me. "Tell me it's not really morning," he says, rubbing his eyes.

"I don't know what time it is," I say. "It's still daylight and I think it's around noon?"

Jace reaches into his pocket, taking out his cell phone to check the time. "Try five-thirty," he says, frowning.

I sigh. "I'm sorry, babe. I feel like we're just sleeping away our honeymoon."

"So, what? It's our honeymoon, we can do what we want." He closes his eyes and presses his lips together. He's so cocky—knowing I'll kiss him with such confidence that he doesn't even look at me. I can't help myself...I lean over and kiss him. When I do, he pulls a ninja move and grabs me around the waist, pulling me on top of him in the bed. I squeal, and kiss him harder.

He nuzzles his face in my neck, trailing soft kisses up my skin until he reaches my ear. "Want to make up for all that time we missed?" he whispers. His throaty voice sends a chill down my spine and sets my insides on fire.

"Yes, sir," I whisper back, positioning my forehead so that it's on top of his. His hands slide down my back, gripping my hips. It's such a dominating grasp—his massive strong hands holding me in place, just inches from my most sensitive parts. I love when he's in control, how he knows everything I like and how he makes sure that making love to him is the greatest thing ever.

But one day I'd like to be the greatest thing to him.

With my legs straddling him on the bed, I lift up onto my hands and give him an alluring smile, pretending at least, that I am in control here. I reach back to my waist, grab his hands with mine and slowly pull them off of me, setting them on the bed. "Aww, but I like touching you," Jace says, frowning.

"Too bad," I say, wiggling my eyebrows. "I'm in charge now. Take off your shirt."

With my bold statement out in the air, Jace pulls off his shirt, tosses it to the floor and repositions himself so that his hands rest behind his head, giving himself a good view. I pull off my shirt and let it fall on top of his. Then I unhook my bra, surprised how nervous I am even though Jace has seen me naked dozens of times. Something about the way his eyes watch me, a mixture of raw desire and admiration flowing from his gaze, sends me into so much anxiety that I want to chicken out. But I don't. I pull off the bra and then slide my hands up his chest, letting my breasts graze against his skin as I kiss his neck.

"Mmm," Jace moans, taking one hand out from behind his head.

"Nope," I snap, taking him by the wrist and pushing his hand back to his head. "No touching. I'm in charge, remember?"

"Aww, that's just mean," he says with a smile that tells me it's anything but mean.

I go back to his neck, kissing it the way he kisses mine, and then lightly trailing my tongue down to his collar bone. His chest tightens when I reach the dip between his shoulder and neck, so I spend extra time on it. With his hands behind his head, his biceps are freaking huge, and the sight of him in all of his shirtless, muscular glory, sends me into a heated lust that might not last long enough for me to keep teasing him.

Slowly, I lift up, letting my breasts touch him again, until I'm sitting up straight while straddling him. I bring my arms together, making sure to press my boobs together, while hiding my stomach, and begin unbuttoning his jeans.

He watches me with a wicked look of desire. His gaze is so strong that I can't look away. When I get his jeans unfastened, he lifts his hips, allowing me to pull them down and out of the way. "You're next," he says, nodding to my shorts.

In the movies, the undressing scenes are always so sexy and well-choreographed. In real life, let's be honest: there is no sexy way to take off your shorts while sitting on top of a guy on the bed.

I roll to the side and try to slip off my shorts as quickly as possible. Despite my stern glare to stay put, Jace breaks the rules and as quickly as I'm undressed, he's rolled over on top of me.

"Hey!" I try to wriggle but he pins me to the bed with his arms on either side of my shoulders. "Not fair! I was supposed to be on top and in charge."

"You are in charge. Every single thing you do drives me completely insane with how badly I want to be inside of you right now." He kisses my breast and then slowly looks into my eyes. "In what way are you not in charge?"

Chapter 8

After what was probably the greatest love making session on earth, Jace and I kick back on our hotel's patio and research touristy places to visit while at the Grand Canyon. I've been feeling a little nauseous in the private jet lately, so although the helicopter tours of the canyon sound amazing, I think it's best to opt out.

Also, the hiking tours that last several hours probably aren't the best, either. These ankles tend to swell after a few hours on my feet. I sigh and hand the tablet back to Jace. "We can't fly in a helicopter, we can't take a hike. This whole pregnancy thing is really bumming me out and ruining our honeymoon."

"Just think of this as a research project. Now we know what they have available, and when our son is old enough to walk and enjoy the sights, we'll come back on a family vacation and do all of these things."

"Well in that case, let me cross gambling in Vegas off the list," I say with a smirk.

"We're not old enough to gamble," Jace says, reminding me of a fact I had totally forgotten. There goes my newly acquired daydream of playing slot machines all night.

Unfortunately, with the reminder that I'm only nineteen, all of my unwanted thoughts from earlier in the week come crashing back into the forefront of my mind. We aren't even old enough to gamble and yet here we are, married and having a kid. A gas station clerk can't sell me a case of beer but I can legally create and bring a brand new human onto this earth. How messed up is that?

Thoughts of those stupid comments I read online about how Jace threw away his life by marrying so young come barreling through my subconscious, reminding me yet again all of the reasons why I should be ashamed of myself.

I'm a career ruiner and soon to be the mother of someone who probably wasn't ready to be born into this life. I should be picking out college applications and buying textbooks and planning which sorority to join.

"What's going on in that mind of yours?"

I look over, eyes wide. How, in just sixty seconds of deep thought, could I have forgotten I was sharing the patio with my husband? "Nothing," I say quickly, throwing him a little smile.

"Nice try," Jace says, reaching over and poking me in the knee. "Seriously, don't be worrying about the stuff you can't do here. We can spend the day bowling in the hotel's bowling alley if you want. I don't mind either way."

"That's not what I'm worried about," I say. Jace smirks and I close my damn mouth before it says another word.

"I know," he says, leaning closer to me. "I just said that shit so you'd deny it and hopefully tell me what's really on your mind."

I groan. "I hate you."

"I love you," he says back in a singsong. "What's wrong, Bayleigh Adams? Is this not the honeymoon of your dreams?"

I shake my head. "It's not that. I mean, it kind of is. But. No."

Jace leans back in his patio chair, hands resting behind his head. "Tell me or I'll tickle you."

I know there's no use in denying him what he wants to know. He'll just get so annoying in his attempts to beg it out of me, that I'll end up telling him anyhow. So, screw it, I think. He's my husband and he kind up gave up the right to be spared all of my worries and thoughts when he married me.

I tell him everything, starting with the tablet snooping and ending with how my biggest fear is that everyone is right and we were idiots by getting married so young.

"That's your biggest fear?" Jace asks once I've finished my monologue of crazed babbling. "Tell me this, Bay. Did you think we were too young to be getting married a week ago?"

I shake my head. "We're young, but I didn't care. If anything, I thought it was romantic because now we can spend our entire lives together."

"Good," Jace says, letting out a breath. "That's how you feel and that's how I feel. So tell me why it hell it matters what someone else thinks? Especially someone on the damn internet?"

I open my mouth but can't think of anything to say. "Well, when you put it like that..." I say, trailing off with a shrug. "I guess it doesn't matter. But I hate reading stuff like that."

He grabs my hand. "Then stop reading it. The day I packed up my shit and went to Salt Gap for the summer was the day I quit reading idiot's opinions on the internet. I haven't looked back and I haven't started caring again since."

"You're right," I say. "As always."

He squeezes my hand and gestures out toward the open air with his other hand. "This is our life. This is me and you. What we do is our own damn business and anyone who tries to give us unsolicited advice can go to hell."

I smile a big, toothy smile. "I like you, Jace Adams."

"Oh, you like me?" He says, his voice flaring with sarcasm. "That's good, I think. Let me consult the internet real quick and see what I should feel about this topic of you liking me..." He lifts the tablet and I grab it out of his hands.

"Oh my God. Way to ruin the moment, you big dork."

His eyes sparkle in the sunlight and it makes my heart go all fluttery in my chest. "Hey, did you know the word dork means a whale penis?"

"Ugh, you're so gross!" I say, followed by, "Wait, seriously?"

He shrugs. "That's what everyone says. Weird, huh?"

I get up from my patio chair and make my way over to his, maneuvering across the tiny balcony so I can sit in his lap. One thing I love about Jace is how any time I get near to him, his body will shift and make room for me, as if by instinct. I never have to ask if I can sit by him, he just lifts his arms and wraps them around me. I don't have to hint that I want a hug, or pucker my lips first—he's always one step ahead of me. Always aware that I'm standing right there, and always happy to give me affection. Those are the reasons I love him.

"I know how we're going to see the Grand Canyon," he says a few moments later.

"How's that?"

"We're going to drive up to the South Rim, find a place to sit and watch the sun set."

I draw in a breath of the warm Arizona air and let my head rest against the front of his chest. "I know it's not hiking or rafting or something crazy," he continues, stroking his fingers through my hair, "But it'll be fun."

I nod. "It'll be perfect."

Chapter 9

Perfect is an understatement. Is there a word that means perfection times a million? Jace opens a bottled water from the cooler we brought and hands it to me. I take a small sip because this moment is so wonderful and I'm not going to ruin it by rushing off to the bathroom. Plus—I look around—I'm not even sure there is a bathroom around here. There are touristy places all over, but Jace and I have ventured far away from where we parked and found an isolated place all to ourselves.

We have a multicolored striped blanket that we purchased from a gift shop spread out on the rocky ground and a Styrofoam cooler, from the same gift shop, filled with drinks and snacks. We wanted to go for that picnic vibe, but as it turned out, there was nothing particularly appetizing to eat at the shop we found. Unless jerky made from exotic animals was your thing.

As a pregnant girl who had, up until now, only ever heard of beef jerky, it was so not my thing.

We sit on the blanket, legs stretched out in front of us as we watch the sun hover around the horizon, making everything glow pinkish-orange. The canyon is without a doubt, the single most beautiful thing I have seen in my life.

I spread out the brochures I had taken from the airport kiosk and read some facts aloud to Jace. "So apparently the canyon is about six million years old, but that's considered pretty young, according to this paper."

"How the hell is that young?" Jace says with a snort.

I keep reading. "Well, the Colorado River has been flowing for seventy million years so I guess the canyon is a little baby in comparison."

"Crazy," Jace says with a shake of his head. "People travel all over the country to come stare at a massive piece of land that would swallow them whole if they fell in...and it's only a baby in Mother Nature years."

"We are so tiny and meaningless on the whole scale of things." I squint my eyes, trying to look as far into the distance as I can, but even with my excellent vision, I can't see the end of the canyon. "Makes you wonder why humans even bother looking at something so massive that all it does is remind us of our insignificance."

"I disagree." He leans back on his hands, letting his head lean over and rest on top of mine. "I think that being reminded of how small we are can help us to truly appreciate everything we have, and the people we love and share it with in this world." He kisses the top of my head and I lean back against his chest.

"I'm happy I share this world with you," I say.

He squeezes me closer. "I wouldn't want it any other way."

Hours later, when the sun has set and we've made it back to our rental car, we're flipping through the GPS, looking for food. "Have you noticed that pretty much all we do when we're together is hang out and eat?" I ask.

Jace gives me a look from the corner of his eye. "We do another thing, too, ya know."

"You know what I mean," I say, sticking out my

tongue. "Sorry we're so boring."

"Nah, you can't think of it like that. One day soon we'll be chasing around a baby all day. I like to just sit back and enjoy my time with you now, while I have it. We have the rest of our lives to be un-boring."

"And then when our kid is grown up and we're retired, we'll go back to being boring," I say, eyes wide with pretend excitement.

He grabs my knee and squeezes it. "Can't wait."

Back at our hotel, we hit up the onsite bowling alley and my new husband gets the luxury of watching my terrible bowling skills. First, I choose a ball from the rack simply because it's a sparkly pink and looks gorgeous under the spinning disco lights.

It has the number sixteen engraved on it next to the bowling alley's logo, and the three holes are so big, I could have fit my big toe inside of them. I hold the heavy ass ball with both of my hands in front of my chest. "Uh, how am I supposed to bowl with this thing?" I ask, watching the lanes next to us to see how the more experienced people do it.

Jace slips his fingers into the ball he chose, which is blue and also has the number sixteen on it. "You should probably get one that's not an extra-large hole size, for starters."

I glance down at the ball again, noticing the XL for the first time. "Hmph," I mutter, walking it back to the rack. Jace steps up to the lane to bowl, doing that little swooshy bowler walk thing, tossing the ball with precision like he's some kind of professional bowler. I stand still near the rack of balls, waiting to see where his ball lands.

Directly in the center of the lane, of course. All but one of the pins fall down with an epic crashing noise and Jace turns around, giving me a lip smirk that means not bad.

It figures that he would be good at bowling. He's good at everything.

I try out the large, medium, and small bowling balls, only to realize that all of the holes are kind of big. Jace laughs when I shove my fingers into a small one, and they go all the way down. "Maybe they have some baby-sized bowling balls around here," he says, looking around.

"Shut up!" I say, but I follow him to the other side of the bowling alley where more racks of balls await. Sure enough, there's an XS ball that fits me perfectly. Of course, when I go to pick it up with my fingers in the holes, I can't lift it.

"Why is this so heavy?" I whine, instinctively scrunching up my face in a way that I know makes me look like a kid.

"Maybe because it's sixteen pounds?" Jace says. "That'll be like twice the size of our baby when he's born. Here, try a twelver."

I frown at the greenish-blue ball he holds out to me. "That's ugly."

"Are bowling balls supposed to be pretty?" he asks, trying to make me take his choice of a ball by pressing it against my arm.

I tilt my head to the side. "It's not pink. It looks like puke."

"Well, we can't have a puke ball, now can we?" Jace says with a laugh. He drops the ball back down to the rack and we spend the next ten minutes searching for a pink extra small, twelve pound ball.

It's the stupid things like this that make me genuinely happy for having married someone like Jace. I know that no other guy I've ever dated would have wasted this much time looking through a bowling alley just to make me happy. And really, I'm not that much of a brat. I don't need a pink ball. But the fact that Jace is willing to do whatever it takes for me just makes me want that ball even more.

Finally we find a pink ball and it's even more sparkly and pink than the first one I found. At only twelve pounds, I can pick it up too, so double win.

Except the magical sparkly pink ball does absolutely nothing in helping me bowl. My ball goes straight in the gutter on my first try. Jace gives me some pointers for my next try, and this time, with his help I get the ball all the way down the aisle and it knocks over two pins on the right.

Oh well, better than nothing.

We bowl several rounds and eat even more nachos, and before long, the alley is completely empty except for us and another couple who look about my mom's age. They're a few lanes down from us and they're both excellent bowlers. I study the woman as she bowls, trying to memorize her fancy foot step pattern so that I can do the same thing. It doesn't exactly work, but I do get better as the night goes on.

When I'm out of soda, I grab Jace's empty cup and mine and head over to the refill station while he bowls. The older woman from a few aisles down walks up behind me, holding an empty pitcher of beer.

"Can't believe it's so dead here tonight," she says, setting down the pitcher and asking the girl behind the counter for another one. "We come here all the time and it's usually packed."

"That's probably for the best," I say back to her. "My terrible bowling would be too embarrassing if more people were here to witness it."

She laughs. "Is this your first time?"

I tell her yes and she nods, understanding. "You'll get better with time. How far along are you?" At first, I'm not sure what she's asking, but then she points to my stomach. "Oh, um, about five and a half months," I say, steeling myself for her reply. I've had the judgement looks and snide comments before. But this is my honeymoon and I'm not going to let her ruin it.

She looks at me incredulously and then smiles. "Wow, you look good for that far along! Girl, I was a freaking whale by three months."

I stand there, shocked for a whole ten seconds. That wasn't rude. It was friendly, even. Sheepishly, I smile back and say, "Thanks. I feel like a whale if that counts for anything."

She laughs and hands the cashier money for her new pitcher. "You're gonna feel a whole lot worse soon, but it'll all be worth it once you get to hold that baby in your arms. Trust me, I have five kids."

"Wow," is the only thing I can think of to say. She walks with me back to our lane, telling me stories of her pregnancies. She doesn't make a single comment about how young I look and when I introduce Jace as my husband, she just shakes his hand and gives him some pointers for dealing with me when I go into labor.

"I like her," I say as she walks back to her lane.

"I can see why," Jace says. "That's like the first

older person who hasn't lectured us on our life choices. Besides our parents, at least."

I nudge him in the ribs. "Not that it matters what people think, right?"

He kisses me on the forehead. "Right."

Chapter 10

Since our sleep schedule is all kinds of weird, I wake up at four in the morning the next day. Not so surprisingly, Jace is awake too. He's watching some show on the hotel's television that's about fixing up old cars. I roll over, snuggling up in our plush hotel comforter and rest my head on his shoulder.

"Good morning, beautiful." I smile at Jace's greeting but don't say anything back due to a massive fear of having morning breath. He holds out a half-eaten Snickers bar. "Want some?"

I lean over and take a bite. As if on cue, Jace knows that the last thing I want to watch is a car mechanic show, so he begins flipping through the channels for something else to watch. Of course, being four in the morning, there's not much on.

"Pretty Woman!" I grab his hand to stop him from scanning channels because the greatest movie ever just appeared on the screen. "Pretty Woman, yes or no?" I ask him, giving my best version of puppy eyes. "Yes?" I nudge him with my elbow. "Yes?"

"If that's what you want," Jace says, rolling his eyes.

Becca and I used to watch this movie all the time because it was one of the only VHS tapes that Mom and I owned when I finally got a TV in my room. I was twelve when Mom found a small TV with a built in VHS player at a garage sale for ten dollars. It was on that glorious day that I finally got a TV in my room. But we didn't have cable, so we had to watch movies. This is where the dusty old Pretty Woman tape became our Friday night movie.

Now that I look back on it, a movie about a

prostitute probably isn't good for twelve year olds to watch. But I didn't care about the first part of it. I loved when Richard Gere's character started falling in love with her, taking her places and making her feel special. That's what kept me coming back to watch it again and again.

"So where do we want to go next?" Jace asks, but it's during the part in the movie where Julia Roberts goes shopping for nice clothes and the sales ladies are total bitches to her, so I don't hear him. He asks again, this time waving his hand in front of my face. "Or do you want to stay here watching this movie you've seen a million times?"

I snap out of the movie's allure, and turn to Jace. "Where do you want to go?" I ask. He shrugs. "Anywhere with you."

"Oh, ha." I lean forward and kiss him. "Now's the time for making decisions, not for being romantic."

Jace's eyes drift off as he tries to think of a place to visit next, and I do the same thing. "Well, most of our trips have revolved around eating," I say with a snort. "Let's go to some famous restaurant or something, or—" My eyes light up and I sit up straight in bed, knocking Jace's arm off my shoulder. "I've got it!"

In the movie Pretty Woman, Richard Gere's character takes her on a dinner date by private jet. They get all dressed up and then fly across the country, have dinner, then fly back to their hotel. I'd always thought the whole thing was flashy as hell—I mean, who has money to take a private jet around as if it were a taxi?—and that was also what made it so special. He cared about her enough to do something so extravagant for her. And, now that I think about it? Isn't that what Jace has been doing for this whole honeymoon?"

"Are you going to keep me waiting forever before you tell me?" Jace asks, poking me in the elbow. "Could we maybe get breakfast first? I'm hungry and something has to be open by now."

"No, you can't eat yet," I say, leaning back to snuggling against him. "I have the perfect idea. Let's eat our breakfast, lunch and dinner Pretty Woman style."

Jace slaps on his goofy joke face and says, "So you want to hire a hooker?"

I roll my eyes. "Nope. I want to fly somewhere different for all three meals today. And maybe tomorrow, too."

He doesn't even need time to think about my idea, which is yet another reason why I love him. "That sounds kickass. Where are we going for breakfast? Oh! Can I suggest somewhere for dinner?"

"I say we hit up a bed and breakfast for breakfast. Don't they usually have really famous breakfast menus? And yes, what's for dinner?" I can't help but smile when Jace leaps out of bed and grabs the tablet to show me his idea for dinner. I love when he gets as into an idea as I am. While he's searching for something on the tablet, he grabs his phone and calls Christopher, our pilot.

"Jace!" I hiss. "It's four-thirty in the morning! You can't call him!"

"Hey, man," Jace says into the phone, blowing me a kiss. "I knew you'd be up since you always get up at four to watch the news," he says into the receiver, more for my benefit I suppose. "We want to hit up a bed and breakfast for breakfast. Do you know any places?" He listens for a moment and then says to me, "Connecticut?"

I nod. "Perfect."

He finishes his phone call, promising that we'll meet him in the hotel lobby in fifteen minutes. I'm not so sure I can have everything packed and ready in that short of a time, but we're both starving and want to get to our breakfast destination as soon as possible.

That's one cool thing about having Christopher fly us around everywhere—Jace has gotten him a hotel room everywhere we've stayed. He said it's customary for a pilot to follow the family they fly for, getting a mini vacation while they're taking their clients on vacation. Apparently Christopher's wife had work that she couldn't get out of, or else Jace would have paid her way, too.

"Hey, can I see that tablet?" I ask all casually, trying not to give myself away.

"That depends...are you going to look up Facebook and see what people are saying about us?"

"No..." The only way I can say this lie is by making an exaggerated guilty face so he knows I'm playing around. Jace hugs the tablet to his chest. "You can look if you have to, but I don't want you to read something stupid and then have it ruin your day."

"You're right," I say, shaking my head. "I don't need to know. I'm having a blast with you and that's all that matters."

The bed and breakfast Christopher flies us to is

absolutely stunning. The entire state of Connecticut in general is beautiful and I can't believe I've never thought to visit it before. Unlike Texas with its hot, dry land, the bed and breakfast is situated between lush woods and cool mountain air. It is a beautiful manor, a mansion if you ask me, that was built in the late eighteen hundreds.

"New England is amazing," I say as we walk up the pathway leading to the mansion's front door. "It's so old and full of history."

"Yeah, Texas and Cali don't have nearly the same feel as this old place." Jace looks around, touching the wooden railing of the porch's stair case. "I bet this place is haunted."

"Maybe we should stay overnight and find out," I say, kidding of course. There's no way I'm sleeping over in a place that's even remotely likely to be haunted.

"Yeah, right. I know you better than to believe you'd do that." Jace shoots me a wink and it's as if he knows what I'm thinking. I guess that's what happens when you find your soul mate—your thoughts are no longer yours because someone else knows you well enough to guess them.

I'm starving by the time we are seated at a table near floor to ceiling windows with a view of the gardens behind the inn. Our table is an antique, with a table cloth and a vase in the center that has a single pink rose. Maybe it's because we're so hungry, but I swear the orange juice here is made from the most divine oranges on earth.

But the orange juice is just a prelude to the breakfast. Jace orders just about everything on the menu and although I'm tempted to join him, I settle for an English muffin with butter, two scrambled eggs, bacon, grits and sliced fruit.

And I eat every single bite of it. Yay for being pregnant!

After breakfast, Jace and I walk hand in hand through the gardens. I take pictures on my phone and hope they come out good enough to be printed and framed when we get home. We find a bench carved out of a fallen tree and we spend the next hour talking about where we should go for lunch. There's so many more options when you get to choose from anywhere in the country.

My phone beeps while we're using it to search for famous restaurants. It's a text from Becca, and although Jace and I had promised we'd ignore our phones for the duration of our honeymoon, Jace nudges me and says, "You should probably see what he wrote. She made this big deal about refusing to text us on our honeymoon and all of that. Maybe it's an emergency."

I slide open the text and find that Jace was sort of right. It's not exactly an emergency, but it's pretty damn close.

"Uh oh," I say, after reading her text twice to make sure I didn't misunderstand it. "Becca and Park are um…" Jace's eyes go wide and I show him the text.

Becca: Yeah so, I'm sorry I'm texting, but Park and I haven't stopped hanging out since the wedding and well…yeah.

"Ah, shit," he says, handing the phone back. "Tell her to run. Run far away!"

The quick rush of excitement I'd had over the idea of my best friend dating my husband's best friend disappears as quickly as it arrived. "But I thought you loved Park? You talk about him all the time."

"Yeah, I love him as a best friend. There's no way in hell I'd let a girl date him though. Especially not your best friend. He's kind of a womanizer who's afraid of commitment."

"Oh." I frown and glance at the phone in my hand. How can I tell her something as crushing as that? Becca is definitely not a one night stand type of girl. She's a commitment girl. A write a guy's name all over her notebook girl. And they've spent the last week and a half together? "This isn't good," I say, and then I remember a very important piece of information. "They're staying at our apartment. You don't think they've…"

"No way," Jace says quickly. "Park would have, but I know Becca and there's no way she'd hook up with him that quickly. I mean, come on." He makes a circular motion with his finger around the top of his head, indicating the imaginary halo that Becca always wears. She's one of the good girls. There's no way she hooked up with Park, because if she did, she'd be even more devastated to learn that he's a player. I probably shouldn't have made all those hints to her on our wedding night. I mean, I didn't really think she'd take me up on the offer to flirt with Park, but it looks like she did.

I sigh and stare at my phone, wishing for the perfect words to tell her that the guy she's crushing on is bad news. After several minutes, I simply type Be careful and press send. Becca knows how to handle herself so I've just got to trust her on this one.

Our lunch plans come to me suddenly. One

moment I'm walking with Jace down the trails behind the inn and the next moment I'm remembering a commercial I saw about a month ago.

"Babe!" I slap his arm in all my excitement and he flinches, making me realize I probably slapped him a little too hard. "I know where we should go to lunch—New York City!"

"Nice. There's tons of places to eat there. What do you have in mind?"

"That place with Japanese food where they cook it in front of you? I heard about it on the radio. The chefs are all crazy about it, like they toss food in the air and stuff? Can we go?" I give him the puppy eyes even though I know he wouldn't tell me no even without my begging face.

"Benihana?" Jace presses his lips together and nods approvingly. "You know that place is all over the country, not just in New York, right?"

"Yes, but I want to see the city," I say, leaning against him as we walk back toward the inn.

"Your wish is my command," Jace says with a cocky air in his voice. "Let's go get some delicious Japanese food.

Chapter 11

The New York City hustle and bustle is probably something I would love—any time that I'm not pregnant. But since I am carrying a mini-Jace in my body, walking through the crowded streets, with their varied and sometimes awful smells, really takes a toll on me. By the time we've eaten dinner, I am so exhausted and weirdly moody that all I want to do is go home.

But you can't tell your husband on week two of your three week honeymoon that you want to go home. So I put on a smile and ask him if we can head to the airport to get some rest in the plane before we fly somewhere for dinner.

"You feeling okay?" he asks. Concern is written all over his face and I hate seeing him worry about me so I nod and roll my eyes like he's crazy for even asking that.

"Of course. I'm just tired."

"Me too. This flying thing is more exhausting than I'd thought it would be. It's almost like we're doing the damn flapping of our wings ourselves."

I laugh at his stupid joke as we flag a taxi to take us back to the private airport just outside of the city. We had invited Christopher to come with us to lunch but he politely declined, saying New York was far too busy of a city for someone like him.

Back in the plane, I check the time—two-thirty in the afternoon. Because of the time zones, it could be lunch or dinner time in wherever we chose to fly to next. But as soon as we board the plane and head toward the bedroom, exhaustion takes over all five of my senses.

You know you're tired when you can taste the sleep as it washes over you.

Jace's laughter wakes me up. I'm in the plane, snuggled under the plush comforter. The smooth vibrations of the plane lets me know we're in the air; which direction we're headed is a mystery. I look over at Jace, who is sitting up in bed next to me, talking on his phone. He's not wearing a shirt and my eyes get caught up in watching his tanned abs flex as he laughs.

Suddenly, without thinking, my hand reaches over and my fingertips slide across his muscular chest. Chills appear on his skin and I drag my hand up to his collar bone and then down his arm, which flexes at my touch. I could admire this man forever. Twenty four hours a day and I'd never get tired of it.

Jace pulls the phone away from his ear, leans down and gives me a quick kiss. "My parents," he whispers, nodding toward the phone. He puts it back to his ear and wraps up the conversation. "I'll tell her," he says, followed by. "Love you too, Mom. Bye."

"You'll tell me what?" I ask, sliding over in bed so I can cuddle closer to him.

"Well," he says, pointing to his fingers as if they are an itemized list. "Dad said to tell you hi and to make sure you're drinking lots of water. For your health I guess. I don't know, I didn't ask. Mom said to tell you she said hi, and then she said I should wake you up so she can tell you herself, but I said I know my wife and she is not a cheerful person if you wake her up."

"Oh, ha, ha," I say, shoving him in the arm, even though he's kind of right.

Jace brushes some hair out of my eyes and tucks it behind my ear. "And then Mom went on and on about the baby clothes she ordered online. She found some dirt bike shirts and like, a pajama set that looks like motocross gear or something."

"Aww, that's cute!" It dawns on me now that I have done very little shopping or planning for the baby. I had wanted to a few times but Jace always told me it'd be easier to plan for the wedding first, and then plan for the baby, so we wouldn't be overwhelmed. Well, now the wedding is over.

"Shit, we should be planning for the baby," I say. "We only have like, three and a half months left until he's here."

"That's plenty of time to set up a nursery," Jace says.

"You sound pretty confident," I say, giving him a look that I didn't know I was capable of until I became a wife. "Exactly how many children have you set up nurseries for?"

"Zero, but, I mean how hard could it be?"

I shrug. "Guess we'll find out."

Jace lifts his arm and wraps it around my shoulders while I snuggle closer, lying on his chest. There's a small flat screen TV facing the bed and he has it on a motocross race on ESPN with the volume down. It's weird to think that if it wasn't for me, Jace would have continued to work hard with his racing and he would have gotten his sponsorships back and continued to be a professional racer. He would have probably been in this race on TV if he had never met me. Motocross is his passion and he had the skills to be one of the best racers in the world. But instead, he chose to settle down in the middle-of-nowhere Texas and just teach motocross to others.

"Do you miss professional racing?" I ask, staring straight ahead at the television. There's no way I could look him in the eye after asking a question like that. "Do you wish you were out there right now in that race?"

"Nope. I'll never quit riding, but I'm not sorry I quit racing."

"Why? You could have been super famous and rich."

"I'm famous and rich enough."

"Yeah, but you could have been more—"

"Bayleigh, there's two things more important in life than being more rich and more famous than I am now."

I look up at him. "What two things?"

"You," he says, leaning down to kiss me. "And our baby."

Even though we're married now, I still feel myself blush. I think he notices it, too, because he kisses my cheek and pulls me into a horizontal bear hug, making me roll on top of him against my will. I have to stay kind of sideways though because my stomach is getting so big. But lying on top of him and his rock-hard chest, with his strong arms wrapped around me completely even though I'm a fat cow right now, is the greatest feeling ever. I feel protected and loved and safe and happy.

My mind wanders back into baby territory. "Now that the wedding is over, I'm kind of super excited to start baby shopping."

"Me too," Jace says. "I didn't realize there was so

much dirt bike themed baby stuff until Mom told me about it. Don't hate me for this, but I'm glad we're having a boy."

"Me too," I say with a sigh of relief. "You can raise him to be an awesome man like you are. I would have no idea what to do with a girl. Except, you know, lock her in her room until she's thirty."

Jace laughs. "I think you'll be a great mom no matter what. But if we were having a girl, I'd probably never let her on a dirt bike. Now I can get our son a bike the day he turns three."

"Three? Um, hell no! Maybe when he's ten he can get a dirt bike."

"Ten? Are you kidding? I was winning national championships at that age."

"We'll talk about this later," I say with a smile. I always knew we'd raise our son to be a dirt bike kid, but three years old is a little too young to give a kid a motorized bike in my opinion. But this is our honeymoon so I'm not going to get in an argument. "So where is this plane headed?"

"You were sleeping pretty hard, so I had to make the choice for us," he says. "You probably don't remember this, but there's this place in Louisiana that—"

"Big Al's Seafood," I say with a laugh. It's a restaurant in Louisiana that Jace's parents always went to when he was a kid and had a race in New Orleans. Jace has talked about their shrimp po'boy sandwiches so many times that he's insane if he thinks I don't remember.

"Is that okay?" he asks. "If not, there's tons of places to eat in New Orleans…"

I nod. "Baby, I love being treated like a princess

all of the time," I say. "Trust me, I do. But you're an equal member in this marriage and you can totally pick the places we go to. So stop looking so worried about your decision. I love it. Let's go."

"You're the best wife ever," he says.

I smile. "You're the best husband ever."

From somewhere in the ceiling, the voice of our pilot crackles through a speaker, "Oh my god, would you two stop being so sappy? I'm getting diabetes by listening to all the sweetness."

Heat rushes up my face as mortification fills every cell of my body. "Wait, you can hear us?" I say aloud, to wherever the microphone is in this room.

"Just for the last minute or two, whenever one of y'all hit the intercom button."

Jace starts laughing and apologizes to Christopher. I jump up out of bed and sure enough, just above our heads is a red button with a label that says intercom. We must have hit it when Jace pulled me on top of him. "Oh my god, I'm so embarrassed," I say, covering my face with my hands.

"I can still hear you," Christopher says. "Hit the button again."

I practically dive through the air to punch the button again, while Jace erupts into laugher. My face is beet red and yet his eyes fill with tears because he's laughing so hard. I grab the pillow and throw it at him.

"You remember that best husband thing I just said? Well, I take it back!"

Jace gives me a seductive look which sends a tingle down my body even though I'm still mad at him. "Imagine if we had hit that button a few hours ago."

I throw the other pillow at him for good measure.

Chapter 12

A few days later, there is one thing I know to be an absolute fact: New Orleans sucks you in and makes you never want to leave. Jace and I found a hotel in the French Quarter and we paid for five nights up front. We were both tired of flying places and Big Al's Seafood really is as delicious as Jace made it out to be, so we wanted to squeeze in as many meals as possible before we go home.

There's something magical about New Orleans, especially at night. The air is thick with history and the people are always nice. And most of them are drunk, but still. They're nice.

I do more shopping in downtown New Orleans than I did in all of Hollywood. We get souvenirs for our parents and for Becca and I buy a dozen more things that I swear are gifts even though I want to keep them for myself.

Between hitting up the zoo and touring several museums, I start to lose myself in thoughts that don't involve our honeymoon. I hadn't thought it would be possible to forget I'm supposed to be on the most romantic adventure of a lifetime, but here I am, touring a Mardi Gras museum with Jace and fretting about motherhood.

We don't have baby stuff yet. We don't have a car seat or bottles or diapers. We have a spare bedroom that's full of junk and a weight bench and a few pairs of Jace's old motocross boots stacked by the window. That's not a nursery.

What's worse than our complete lack of preparedness to bring a child into the world? The fact that we haven't chosen a name for him yet.

It's weird, right? We're having a baby, and we've known that for almost six months and we still haven't talked about what we should name him. I thought for sure after the wedding, Jace would bring it up. He was so adamant about only allowing ourselves a small amount of stress for the wedding, and leaving the baby stuff for after. Well, now it's after. It's been two weeks. I am ready to stress about this now.

Why haven't we talked about it? And why is this such a weird topic? I mean, we're having a kid together. I should be able to just bring it up. Just say hey Jace, what should we name our kid?

I guess that deep down I'm scared. Worried he'll want a name I don't like, or vice versa. I haven't really put a lot of thought into the idea myself, which I know is crazy because most girls have their future kid's names pick out before they're even conceived. But it's never really been a big deal with me. I'm not even sure I wanted kids before I met Jace. And now that we accidently got pregnant, I'm so excited I can't stand it. Now, I can't picture a life where it isn't Jace, me, and our son.

But that son needs a name and I need to talk to my husband about this. Come on, Bayleigh. You can do this.

Big Al's Seafood has the world's greatest hushpuppies. It doesn't say that on their menu or anything, but I have given myself the authority to declare them the greatest hushpuppies in the entire world. I've never liked them before in any other restaurant, but here, they're to die for. Golden little balls of cornbread and seasoning and whatever the hell else they use to make them. They're amazing.

"I can't believe you ordered a basket of hushpuppies for lunch," Jace says as he takes a massive bite of his po'boy sandwich.

"I also ordered a Coke," I say, lifting up the glass to give it credit. "I can't help myself. They are too good to be the side to an entrée. They should be an entrée all by themselves."

"I'm pretty sure there's no protein in those things, so they make an awful meal."

"You make an awful meal!" I stick out my tongue playfully and he rolls his eyes. "Besides," I say, finding a way to bring up the topic that's been bugging me. "I'm a pregnant lady with weirdo pregnancy cravings so you just have to put up with me and do what I say. And if I want to order twenty hushpuppies and eat them all in one sitting, I will."

Jace raises his Dr. Pepper in a salute to my declaration of food love. "Damn straight," he says. "Eat up. I want my son to be big and strong and kickass like me."

Okay, now's the time. "Yeah, so about that," I say in an incredible display of being not the least bit smooth about it. "What should we name our son? We're running out of time to decide on something."

His expression turns thoughtful and I'm glad, because this is something he should be thinking about. "What did you have in mind?"

I shrug. "I don't know. What about you?"

"Seriously?" His head cocks to the side as he studies me. I shrug. "Yeah?"

"I don't know, I just assumed you had like fifty names picked out already."

I frown, feeling like a terrible mom-to-be. "Not really," I admit. "I mean, I think about how we need a name but I never think of what we should name him. Honestly, I've been wondering what you think."

Jace finishes his sandwich in one massive bite and I have to give him credit because the boy can eat a ton of food in record time. Maybe we should enter him into eating contests — that can be his new claim to fame besides the motocross world. "Am I total asshole if I say I haven't really thought about it? I just kind of assumed you'd pick the name and tell me when you knew it."

"Why does it have to be all on me?" I ask.

He shrugs. "Because you're my woman and I trust you to make these kinds of decisions."

I realize I've been tearing my napkin into tiny pieces. "I don't know, Jace." I have more to say, but an overwhelming feeling of sadness falls over me like a thick blanket. Suddenly all I can do is stare at the table and try swallowing the lump in my throat.

"Baby, what's wrong?" I feel his warm hand touch mine, his fingers closing over mine so I can't keep tearing the napkin. "Please talk to me."

"I don't know, I guess…" Words come out of my mouth but they're just placeholders for what I really want to say. "I don't know. It's nothing. Just…forget it."

I stab into a hushpuppy with my fork and eat it. If my mouth is full then I can't talk.

"Honey, what happened? Why are you suddenly upset? Talk to me."

I don't look up at him because I know if I do, then I'll see his face and his sincere eyes and that little wrinkle he gets in the middle of his forehead when he's worried about me. I can't see any of that because then I might cry and I can't cry in the middle of freaking Big Al's Seafood. So I just shake my head and make this little smile and blame it on the pregnancy hormones.

Jace accepts my excuse even though we both know it's a lie.

Chapter 13

We're back on the plane. Headed to Florida. There's less than a week left of our honeymoon and I said it would be fun to visit the beaches of the east coast since we've seen the west coast and we live near the beaches in Texas. Jace agreed and he seems really excited about this destination. He wanted to visit Disney World but as the days go on and my belly gets bigger, so do my ankles. Walking around in the hot sun all day doesn't seem fun, so I promised him we'd take another trip to Disney World when our kid is older. For now, I just wanted to lounge on a beach.

I'm pretty sure every beach is better than the beaches in Texas. Our sand is covered in seaweed and the water is muddy brown with the constant warnings of jellyfish posted everywhere. Miami should be fun. A relaxing way to end the summer and our honeymoon.

I haven't spoken about the baby naming thing. Although it plagued me on the inside, I shoved the thoughts away, buried them deep in my subconscious and just tried to have fun with Jace. As much fun as it was seeing new hotels and shopping in new stores and eating food at all kinds of places, my body was tired and my mind was driving itself crazy thinking about baby names.

The name we chose for our son would have to live with him forever. It would need to sound good paired with the last name Adams. It would need to be something that a girl could scribble on her notebook in fifteen years. I smile at the thought of our son having a girlfriend in the future. I bet Jace would teach him how to treat a girl. He wouldn't be like Ian or any of the other assholes in my past. He'd be a mini version of the greatest man on earth—my husband.

"What ya smiling about?" Jace nudges me from his seat in the airplane. We're preparing to land so Christopher had us buckle up. My smile quickly fades as we begin the descent. Even after making several stops in our rented private jet, the feeling of landing always makes my stomach seize up uncomfortably, like when you make the drop on a roller coaster. I grab the armrest and take a deep breath.

Jace laughs. "Okay, the smile is gone." The plane makes a deep descent as the landing strip gets nearer and nearer and then Jace's head bobs as we touch the ground. "Man, I hate that," he says, reaching over and grabbing my hand. "I don't know how pilots do it all the time."

"Me neither," I say, feeling a wave of relief wash over me as the plane comes to a stop. We unbuckle our seatbelts and I rush to get to the side door before Jace does, since it's fun to be the first one out of the plane. It's become our little contest with each landing we do, and lately I've been winning.

"Don't think you're getting out of answering my question," Jace says into my ear as we step off the plane.

"What question?"

"The reason you were smiling back there. It looked like whatever was going on in your head was pretty good."

I reach up and kiss him, threading my fingers through his hair. "I'll tell you later."

The beaches of Florida are where it's at. Seriously. Best beaches ever. Jace and I rented a car and stopped at the first place we found after leaving the Fort Lauderdale airport. It was an apartment complex, a nice one, with a crazy beautiful view of the shore.

"Why are we stopping here again?" Jace asks as I yank of my seat belt and bolt out of the rental car.

I bend down and take off my shoes, tossing them into the floorboard. "I need the sand in my toes," I say as an explanation. The wind blows through my hair and it's warm and it's sunny and this is the most gorgeous place we've been.

Maybe not as gorgeous as the Grand Canyon, but it's perfect in its own way. I take off running through the parking lot of an apartment complex we don't belong to, past some picnic tables and straight to the sand. Jace is behind me, his feet splashing into the water just a second after mine.

"Wow," I say, mesmerized. Unlike in California, this water isn't cold. And unlike at home, the water isn't brown. It's warm and crystal clear and I can see my pink toenail polish sparkling up at me through the water.

It's just after noon and there's a ton of people outside enjoying the beach like we are. But all I care about is Jace and me, here and now, in our own little world. We stand in the water about calf-deep and I lift my arms up and around Jace's neck. He grabs my waist, his fingers lacing together around my blue sundress.

"This place is amazing," I say, wiggling my toes

as I look up at him. The sand here isn't like the sand back home. It's thick, chunky and super soft. The only thing around is sand and water, no dirt or debris or old tires. This is the perfect beach.

"We should have come here first," he says, looking out over the horizon. "The weather is perfect."

I nod, thinking it's a little bit humid but I'm not going to say that and ruin the mood. "Let's find a hotel right on the water like this."

Jace looks around and lets go of my waist, grabbing my hand instead. "What about that place?" he says, pointing to a Hilton just down the beach.

"Well, that was easy," I say. "What should we do now?"

Jace grabs the beach bag from his arm, and I can't believe I hadn't noticed that he grabbed it until now. He takes out a beach towel and spreads it out on the sand. I sit in front of him, facing the shore. He wraps his arms around me and I lean back into his chest, taking deep breaths so that I can forever remember the smell of the beach and the feeling of these perfect little moments with him.

"So what were you smiling about?" he asks after a few moments of serene silence.

"I was thinking about how our son will grow up to be just like you, and how happy that makes me."

He chuckles. "I guess that's a good thing. Think you can handle two of us?"

"Jace—" I take a deep breath and tell myself that now is the time. "It bothers me that you don't seem to care about what we should name him. I mean, it's your baby too. Why don't you care?"

I look up and back at him and he frowns. "I'm

sorry, Bay. I didn't mean for it to sound like that. I do care. I just, I figured you'd pick a name."

"I want you to pick a name with me, not just settle for whatever I come up with," I say, running my fingers through the sand. "I don't want to be the wife that makes all the decisions. We should be a team."

"We are a team, babe."

I turn back to look at him and the wind blows my hair all in my face. Jace brushes it back, gently tucking the strands behind my ear. "I'm sorry I left you to decide by yourself. Let's do this now. Let's figure out our kid's name."

I sit up and turn to face him. "Really? What do you have in mind?"

Jace's lips move to the side of his mouth. "Umm…how about…"

I sigh. "Every name I can think of reminds me of some celebrity with that name, or of a character from a book. I want something unique. Something that doesn't remind us of anything else."

He nods. "I like the letter J. Anything that starts with a J would be cool. Like maybe…" He goes back to thinking, his eyes looking up at the clouds.

I look down at the sand, running my fingers through it over and over again as I think of names that start with the letter J. It's a good idea, the J thing. I like it, and I want to pick a name now more than ever.

"I guess we don't have to decide right away," Jace says after a few moments go by and we've both got nothing.

"Yes, yes we do. I've been fretting about this for months now. Let's pick a name now, and let's get it over with. Then we can tell our son we named him while on the greatest honeymoon ever."

"Good idea. Maybe we can think of a name that reminds us of this trip…"

My eyes light up at the idea. "I love it!" I say. "What's a J name that will always make us think of our honeymoon?"

Our eyes meet and then mine light up at the same time Jace's does. I've got an idea, and he does too. "Jet!" I blurt out, wanting to get my idea out before he says his.

Only, I'm not faster than he is because he yells the same name at the same time. "Oh my God, did we just think of the same name?" I say, feeling a rush of excitement run through my veins.

"Did you say Jet? Because I said Jet."

I nod. "The best part of our trip was the private jet. Jet starts with J. And let's face it, Jet is a badass name."

"Perfect for our little badass," he says, leaning forward to put his palm on my stomach. As if adding to the conversation himself, our baby rolls over and kicks his leg out, pressing against Jace's hand. I melt a little inside when I see the way his entire face morphs into an expression of love I've never seen him have before. "That's my little man," he says to my stomach. "You're my little Jet."

"I can't wait to meet you," Jace whispers, his attention still focused on Jet. I smile as I watch him gaze lovingly at my stomach, moving his hands around to catch the little flutters of movement. This man, with his giant muscles and scars from crashing dirt bikes and failed dare-devil attempts, is a total sap when he's with me. He's cuddly and loving but hard and protective at the same time.

I get chills even in the dead of summer when it's scorching hot out here. The feeling of Jace's hand on my stomach, with our unborn baby moving around between us, is such a powerful display of love. Tears flood my eyes and fall down my cheeks. I have never been so in love in my entire life. I have never been so happy. So content. So excited for what's to come.

In this moment, with my husband sitting next to me, resting his hands on my stomach, his eyes lighting up every time he feels a movement, with the sun overhead and the sound of waves crashing ashore, I know that everything is going to be perfect.

My life is perfect. Right here, right now, and forever.

###

About the Author

Amy Sparling is the author of The Summer Unplugged Series, The Devin and Tobey Series, Deadbeat & other awesome books for younger teens. She also writes books for older teens under the pen name Cheyanne Young. She lives in Houston, Texas with her family and a super spoiled rotten puppy.

Amy loves getting messages from her readers and responds to every single one! Connect with her on one of the links below.

Connect with Amy online!

Website: http://www.AmySparling.com
Twitter: https://twitter.com/Amy_Sparling
Instagram: http://instagram.com/writeamysparling
https://www.authorgraph.com/authors/Amy_Sparling
Wattpad:
http://www.wattpad.com/user/AmySparlingWrites

Printed in Poland
by Amazon Fulfillment
Poland Sp. z o.o., Wrocław

14230033R00048